Jingle Baba

The Happiest Camel

Notes to the Reader

"Bright"—Heart-Master Adi Da, the unique Spiritual Master and World-Friend, used the word "Bright" to refer to the Divine Reality that is the Condition of every one and every thing. Even as a child, as soon as He acquired the capability of language, He called His own Divine Condition "the 'Bright'", which had been apparent to Him since His infancy.

Divine—The Condition in which we and all beings are arising; the Free Condition.

Heart-Master—One who has fully realized the Divine Reality and who lives as that Reality all the time.

Names of the non-humans—All the names of the animals in this book were given to them by Heart-Master Adi Da Himself.

Book and cover design by Leslie Waltzer, www.CrowfootDesign.com
Cover photos by the author

Photo Credits

The photographs in this book were drawn from the collections of Ron Jensen (3, 15, 16, 17, 19, 28); Lena Jenkins (30); Ruy Carpenter (41 top); Andrea Keningston (43 top, 45); Jake Siglain (46 top, 48, 49 top); Sandra Gutman (47); and the author (front and back covers, 9, 12, 13, 31, 32, 33, 34, 35, 36 left, 40, 41 bot., 42, 43 bot., 44 top, 44 bot., 46 bot., 49 bot., 50, 51, 52, 62). Images owned by The Avataric Samrajya of Adidam Pty Ltd, as trustee for The Avataric Samrajya of Adidam, used by permission.

ISBN 978-1-54395-318-3

**All profit from the sale of this book will be donated to the ongoing care and support
of the sacred camel herd and the other non-humans at Fear-No-More Zoo.**

Jingle Baba
The Happiest Camel

By Rita Gordon Siglain
Based on a True Story

LETTING GO PRESS
Middletown, California

Heart-Master Adi Da with the author and her dog

For my Beloved Heart-Master
Adi Da Samraj, in gratitude and love.

One day, the Great Heart-Master Adi Da said
to His devotees that He would like a camel for
His Zoo on the Mountain Of Attention Sanctuary.

His devotees began looking all over the world
for a baby camel, and soon they found a friendly
little camel, only one year old, at the London Zoo.
So they sent a picture of him to Heart-Master Adi Da.

The "Bright" Heart-Master was now residing on His beautiful, most sacred Sanctuary in Fiji, where He often did His Great Blessing-Work. He looked at the picture of the little camel a long, long time. He was very pleased. He named him "Jingle Baba".

And so devotees brought Jingle Baba to Fear-No-More,
Heart-Master Adi Da's sacred Zoo on the Mountain
Of Attention Sanctuary in California.

He loved growing up at this happy place, where he could relax on the grass and feel the Great Divine Oneness. Heart-Master Adi Da made sure that he had plenty of space, with lots of fresh air and sunshine.

For the first time in his life, Jingle Baba
was free to roam around on his own.

He made friends everywhere!

But when would he meet Heart-Master Adi Da?

Six years had gone by. Jingle Baba was getting bigger.

Then suddenly one day, Heart-Master Adi Da
returned to the Mountain Of Attention Sanctuary
and went to meet His Jingle Baba at last.

He loved the gentle camel. He petted him on his nose
and head and gave him His Great Blessing Regard.

All of a sudden Jingle Baba started moving around and shaking with excitement. He almost fell over! He could feel the Master's "Bright" Heart-Happiness, and he loved Him right away.

From that day on, whenever Heart-Master Adi Da
stayed on the Mountain Of Attention Sanctuary
He spent a lot of time with Jingle Baba. He'd often
feed him tasty treats and simply enjoy his company.

He liked having Jingle Baba around Him so much that
He said to His devotees, "Jingle Baba has to live at the Zoo
because he's so big, but if he were really small, like a frog
or a lizard, I'd have him live in My house with Me!"

Jingle Baba was growing up fast. Soon he was a 2000-pound giant!
Heart-Master Adi Da knew it was time to give him a special gift . . .

A lady camel to be with! She was a beautiful camel with big googly eyes.
Heart-Master Adi Da named her **"Google Mama"**!

Before long, Google Mama and Jingle Baba started having little camels of their own! Heart-Master Adi Da named them **"Peaceful Baba"** . . .

. . . **"Purnimama"** . . .

. . . and **"Jelly Baba"**.

Jingle Baba loved his children . . .

. . . and his sweet companion Google Mama.

But he loved NOTHING MORE than
seeing Heart-Master Adi Da at the Zoo!

Then one morning, as it sometimes happened,
Heart-Master Adi Da left the Sanctuary suddenly.
No one knew when He would return.

Several months went by. Jingle Baba really missed Him.
"Where could He BE?" he wondered. He wanted to see his Beloved
Guru Adi Da again, and so he set out on his own to find Him!

He wandered over to the Manner of Flowers, Heart-Master
Adi Da's home. He waited outside the gate, looking back and
forth in every direction. But Jingle Baba didn't see Him.

So he went to look in the Zoo. He found his buddies Gunther and Pickles, the pot-bellied pigs who were napping in the dirt. Gunther snorted a few times to greet him. Jingle Baba asked, "Have you seen Heart-Master Adi Da?" But the pigs just went back to sleep!

He went nearby to Yes and No, the two giant tortoises who were warming themselves in the sun. When they picked up their heads to look at him he asked, "Have you seen Heart-Master Adi Da?" But Yes and No just moved slowly toward some food!

He wandered over to Snooze, the white cockatoo who was flying around merrily. "Have you seen Heart-Master Adi Da?" he asked. But Snooze just kept showing off his yellow head-feathers!

Of course, Jingle Baba could not forget tiny Stim,

the green chameleon who was climbing branches.

"Stim, have you seen Heart-Master Adi Da?"

he asked. But Stim simply went on climbing!

So Jingle Baba visited Tut, the friendly llama
who was enjoying a good treat from a friend. "Tut",
Jingle Baba said, "Have you seen Heart-Master Adi Da today?"
But Tut was hungry. He didn't even look up!

And so Jingle Baba went down the long trail to Drench and H2O,

the mini horses who were grazing peacefully on the grass.

He asked, "Have you seen Heart-Master Adi Da?"

But the minis just kept on grazing!

At last, Jingle Baba found giant Walla Kazoo, the security dog
who went EVERYWHERE on the Sanctuary.
Surely HE would know where Heart-Master Adi Da was!

"Have you seen Heart-Master Adi Da?" Jingle Baba asked.
But Walla Kazoo just lay down and scratched his back
in the grass. He hadn't seen Him either!

For three days in a row, Jingle Baba went looking for Heart-Master Adi Da.
When he had looked so much that he couldn't look any more,
he relaxed. He took a quiet walk with his daughter, Purnimama.

He munched on some hay with his family of camels.

But then Jingle Baba saw someone coming towards him who seemed as big and "Bright" as the sun. It was Heart-Master Adi Da!

The Divine Heart-Master petted Jingle Baba and fed him some sweet bananas.

"Hello, Jingle Baba," He said in His deep, beautiful voice.

Jingle Baba was very calm and very still.

Then Heart-Master Adi Da held Jingle Baba's giant head
in His hands. He looked at Jingle Baba a long time.

Jingle Baba looked at Heart-Master Adi Da, too.

He felt his Master's Great Love.

And he was the happiest camel there ever was!

"At heart, all are one."

Heart-Master Adi Da was born Completely Happy and Free. Even as a young child He was only Conscious Light Itself, the "Bright", and He loved so profoundly that He wanted all beings to live as the "Bright", too.

He once said,

> *At heart, a human being is not the slightest bit different from the reptiles, the birds, the former dinosaurs, the elephants, the plants, the trees, the wind, the sky, the microbes.*

I do not make the slightest jot of distinction between a human being and any other form or appearance.

I am in Conversation with all beings and things.

If you examine beings other than the human—feel them, are sensitive to them, enter directly into relationship with them—you discover that they are the same.

All is One. All are the same.

All equally require Divine Compassion, Love, and Blessing. All.

Thousands of stories can be told of Heart-Master Adi Da's profound Love and Compassion for all beings. This story for children about Heart-Master Adi Da and His camel Jingle Baba is one such story. May all be moved at the heart by His Divine Play.

Acknowledgements

Jingle Baba, the Happiest Camel has been a labor of love for over 13 years. It could not have been published without the help and support of many, many people.

Most especially I wish to thank my Beloved Heart-Master Adi Da Samraj, whose profound Love and Compassion for all beings, both human and non-human, drew me to His Great Divine Heart. In 2005, when He graciously reviewed the first version of the story and offered instructions and suggestions, I vowed to complete the book no matter what it took. Words cannot describe my gratitude and my love for You.

I also wish to thank my dear husband, Jake Siglain, with all my heart. Without you this book would never have been possible. Your incredible patience and love over the years, as well as the countless hours you spent giving me your honest, often brilliant feedback and suggestions, have been invaluable and the greatest support. I love you.

I also deeply thank the following:

Ruchiradama Quandra Sukhapur of the Ruchira Sannyasin Order of Adidam Ruchiradam, for your guidance, encouragement, sensitivity, and care.

Ruchiradama Nadikanta, for your passion for Fear-No-More Zoo and for being so available to talk about the camels through the years.

Megan Anderson and Jonathan Condit at The Dawn Horse Press, for your skillful editorial reviews of the manuscript and your help during the many phases of development of the book. Megan, I cannot praise you and thank you enough for your support, guidance, and love.

Matt Barna, dedicated and brilliant art director at The Dawn Horse Press, for your incredible help finding photographs and your expertise in preparing the photographs for print.

Leslie Waltzer, for your beautiful cover and book design, for generously donating half your time, for your genius, your friendship, and for your great spirit.

James Minkin, production manager at The Dawn Horse Press, for your guidance and expertise about printing processes and printers, and for always being there to talk to.

Scott Campbell of Sacred Archives—there are no words to describe my gratitude for all your help finding and preparing photos for the book from the Sacred Archives of Adidam.

Naamleela Free Jones, for your astute editing and fine-tuning of the manuscript through its early stages.

Sara Tourtellotte, for your support and friendship, and for your passionate and skillful care of the camels and the other non-humans at Fear-No-More Zoo, as well as your relentless dedication. It is an honor to serve there with you.

Stuart Camps, for your service to Jingle Baba and the other camels, as well as all the other non-humans at Fear-No-More Zoo, and for your helpful review of the book manuscript in its early stages.

Glen Johannes, for the sweet tales you often shared with me about Jingle Baba's early life.

Ron Jensen, for the many photographs of Jingle Baba you gave me and for your stories about Jingle Baba.

The friends who previewed the book, for your invaluable feedback: Olivia Spence, Patricia Royman, Raewyn Bowmar, Bonnie Siniakin, Judith Parkinson and her young grand-daughter Sydney, Kerry Faithful, and Harp Gerakin.

Nick Elias, for helping with some of the photographs, and for sending me the beautiful one you took on page 39.

Ren-ai Lindley, for your help with photograph permissions and copyright issues. Thank you so much.

The many friends, too numerous to mention, who believed in the project and offered financial support. I am so grateful. This couldn't have happened without you.

My seven grandchildren, Kelsea, Brooke, Billy, Kayla, Dylan, Leo, and Lila, whose young, beautiful faces inspired me over the years to stick with it despite difficulty. A special thanks to Leo and Lila Blum, who let me read the story to them again and again and gave me wonderful feedback. I love all of you so much.

My beloved dog Roxanne, a loyal and most beautiful friend, who was the best listener of all.

And finally, the happy and mighty camel Jingle Baba, who demonstrated such devotion and sensitivity to Bhagavan Adi Da that Bhagavan called him His "Messenger". Week after week Jingle Baba allowed me to be alone with him and his family in their close, inner circle, taking hundreds of photos of them and getting to know them. Some of those photos appear in this book.

At the Sacred Camel Gardens of Fear-No-More Zoo,
on a most beautiful, private Sanctuary in Northern California,
we now have a large herd of awesome camels, many of whom
are direct descendants of the camel Jingle Baba.
To find out more about them, please visit
www.facebook.com/JingleBabaMama

To learn more about the life and work of Avatar Adi Da Samraj, please visit
www.adidam.org

To purchase books by and about Avatar Adi Da, please visit
www.dawnhorsepress.com